Mel Bay's Deluxe
Harmonica Method

A Thorough Study for the Indiviual or Group

By Phil Duncan

CD Contents

This book is available either by itself or packaged with a companion audio and/or video recording. If you have purchased the book only, you may wish to purchase the recordings separately. The publisher strongly recommends using a recording along with the text to assure accuracy of interpretation and make learning easier and more enjoyable.

1 2 3 4 5 6 7 8 9 0

Visit us on the Web at www.melbay.com — E-mail us at email@melbay.com

Foreword

To the student:

This book is designed as a thorough step by step instruction on the "10" hole harmonica. This comprehensive book explains musical techniques with playing techniques. The playing of the "10" hole harmonica can be achieved by playing each song and exercise as presented in this book. This book's purpose is to help combat the trial and error of playing the harmonica, and puts the playing of the harmonica in the reach of everyone. It is suggested by the author that each harmonica student seek out a music instructor to further help eliminate errors.

Philip Duncan

To the teacher:

This book will guide the harmonica teacher, or, in fact, any music teacher, with exercises and an array of pieces that have been adapted specifically for the "10" hole harmonica. It is surprising that in the long history of harmonica; the teaching of harmonica as "formal education" is still controversial. In bygone days the harmonica player gained experience in the everyday challenges of creating music. He learned from his fellow players and he had time for trial and error while trying out new ideas at the risk of failing. But with the fast pace of today these opportunities are virtually non-existent. In any event, a book such as this one fills the gap by organizing the "learning process" by steps so as to minimize the errors on the road to achievement. With the guidance of a music teacher the errors can virtually be eliminated.

Philip Duncan

Musical Contents

Introduction

There are two types of harmonicas, the chromatic and diatonic. This book will use the diatonic harmonica ONLY. Specifically, it will use the TEN-HOLE Harmonica in the key of "C".

How To Hold The Harmonica

Hold the harmonica firmly in the left hand with hole number one to the left. The left index and middle fingers should lie along the upper part of the instrument and the thumb along the lower part. The right hand should be cupped around the back side of the harmonica.

Care Of The Harmonica

Depending on how much it is used, the instrument will eventually deteriorate and some of the reeds will either get stuck or play out of tune. If you live in a big city you may find a repair shop that can restore a worn out harmonica. Probably it would be best, however, just to purchase a new one.

Carefully avoid playing the harmonica after eating. Food particles will stop the reeds from playing. Always slap the harmonica on the palm of the hand to clear any saliva or foreign particles that may be in the instrument. Many players soak their harmonicas in water before playing. This makes wood harmonicas swell, giving an air tight fit. This means that more sound can be produced with less effort. After the instrument is soaked, the excess water must be removed by tapping the harmonica on the palm of the hand. Repeated soaking of the wood harmonicas will cause the wood parts to swell permanently. It will be necessary to trim the wood that comes in contact with the mouth. This can be done with a sharp knife.

Producing The Single Tone

Sounds are produced by blowing the breath through the instrument or by drawing the breath through the instrument. To produce a single tone, place the harmoica comfortably in your mouth as though to blow four holes. Now bring your tongue forward so that it covers three holes on the left.* This should leave only one hole at the right of your mouth uncovered. Make sure you don't blow into more than one hole at a time. Keep your lips and tongue in the same position and blow, then draw the breath. DON'T LET AIR ESCAPE THROUGH THE SIDES OF YOUR MOUTH. BLOW AND DRAW T-H-R-O-U-G-H the harmonica not at it.

*Note: Place tongue on ALL Holes, then move the tongue to the left until ONE single tone is produced.

Tongue Blocks 3 holes,
Sixth hole sounds.

Vibrato

You may change the sound of your playing by adding a wavering tone, called VIBRATO. Holding the harmonica in the left hand, close the right hand over the left and by opening and closing the right hand, the wavering of the tone will begin. As the right hand is moved to and from, slowly, a rich mellow vibrato is the result. By moving the right hand quickly the wavering of the tone increases. The heel of both hands stay in contact with each other while the fingers of the right hand move back and forth in unison. The movement of the fingers should be smooth and even.

Example

Breathing

The key to breathing is to breathe like a swimmer. In other words, you should breathe in the mouth and out the nose. This helps to exhale the excess air in your lungs on difficult passages. Don't let air escape through the sides of your mouth. Aim your breath THROUGH the harmonica not at it. You are ready for the excercises and pieces on the following pages.
NOTE: Always COUNT THE TIME (Beats per measure) REMEMBER TO TAP YOUR FOOT TO EACH BEAT.

Chapter I
Music for the "10" Hole Harmonica

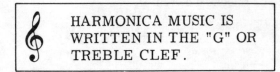

HARMONICA MUSIC IS
WRITTEN IN THE "G" OR
TREBLE CLEF.

THE MUSIC STAFF

Staff   Some notes   Some notes
               are line notes   are space notes

space
above

space
below

All notes are either line notes or space notes

Study the following notes and mark them ☐L or ☐S for line or space.

Study the following notes and write the number of the line or space.

This is a whole note. **o** In most music the whole note recieves 4 counts or beats. The sound must last 4 counts or beats.

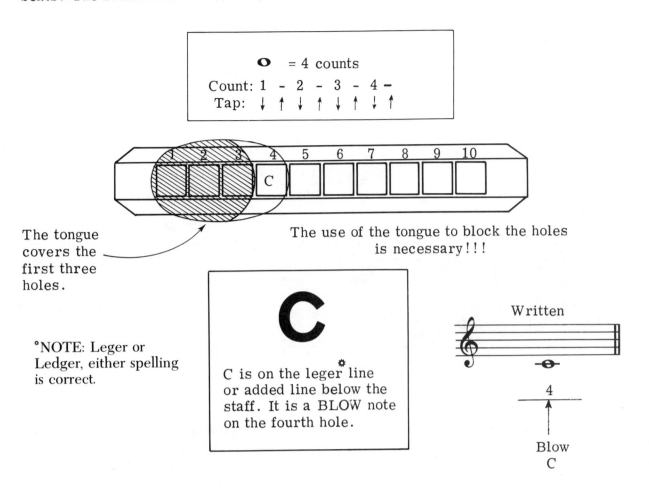

o = 4 counts

Count: 1 - 2 - 3 - 4 -

Tap: ↓ ↑ ↓ ↑ ↓ ↑ ↓ ↑

The tongue covers the first three holes.

The use of the tongue to block the holes is necessary!!!

°NOTE: Leger or Ledger, either spelling is correct.

C

C is on the leger° line or added line below the staff. It is a BLOW note on the fourth hole.

Written

4

Blow
C

① 4 counts per measure

(Blow note, hole four)

Double bar end of piece

(Hold....)

Count: 1 - 2 - 3 - 4 -

Tap foot: ↓ ↑ ↓ ↑ ↓ ↑ ↓ ↑

tap tap tap tap

Two dots means to repeat piece.

4   4   4   4

This is a half note. ♩ In most music the half note recieves 2 counts or beats. The sound must last 2 counts or beats.

$$\text{♩} = 2 \text{ counts}$$

Count: 1 - 2 -
Tap foot: ↓ ↑ ↓ ↑

Down Up Down Up

Count: 1 - 2 - 3 - 4 -
Tap foot: ↓ ↑ ↓ ↑ ↓ ↑ ↓ ↑

Repeat

MUSICAL MEASURE

Measure and bars

Measure bar

(Measure)

This line has 4 measures.

1   2   3   4

Double bar

How many measures are there in this line?

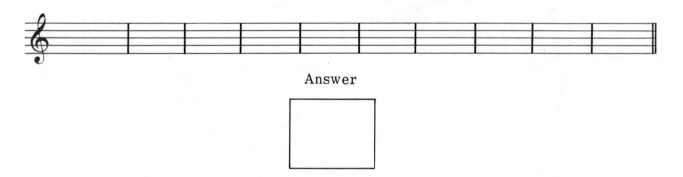

Answer

The tongue covers the first three holes.

Draw

D

D is on the space below the staff. It is the DRAW note on the 4th hole of the harmonica.

Written

4 ↓

Draw

③ (Draw)   (Blow)

Repeat

Count: 1 - 2 - 3 - 4 -
Tap: ↓ ↑ ↓ ↑ ↓ ↑ ↓ ↑

4↓ 4↓ 4↓ 4↑ 4↑ 4↑

④

Count: 1 - 2 - 3 - 4 -

4↓ 4↓ 4↓ 4↑ 4↓ 4↑ 4↑

⑤

Count: 1 - 2 - 3 - 4 -

4↑ 4↓ 4↓ 4↑ 4↓ 4↑

REMEMBER: ALWAYS TAP THE FOOT!

This is a quarter note. ♩ In most music the quarter note recieves one count or beat. The sound lasts only one count or beat.

♩ = 1 count

Count: 1 -
Tap foot: ↓ ↑

Review:

o   Whole note = 4 counts

♩   Half note = 2 counts

♩   Quarter note = 1 count

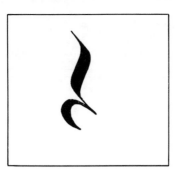

Quarter Rest

⑧ The quarter rest is one count of silence. (No air through the harmonica)

Count: 1 - 2 - 3 - 4 -
Sound   Silence   2 - 3 -
                                    Silence

⑨

Count: 1 - 2 - 3 - 4 -
Tap foot: ↑ ↓ ↑ ↓ ↑ ↓ ↑ ↓

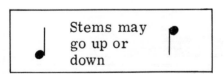

How the notes are placed on the musical staff.

| Below the middle line the stem turns up | Middle line Stems may go up or down | Above the middle line the stems goes down |

11

Change these whole notes to quarter notes:

The tongue covers
the 2nd, 3rd, & 4th holes

Blow

E

E is on the bottom
line of the musical
staff. It is the
<u>BLOW</u> note in the
5th hole of the harmonica.

Written

E
5

Blow

⑩ Blow note hole 5

Count: 1 - 2 - 3 - 4 - 1 - 2 - 3 - 4 - 1 - 2 - 3 - 4 -
Tap foot: ↓ ↑ ↓ ↑ ↓ ↑ ↓ ↑

5   5   5   5 5 5 5   5

⑪

Count: 1 - 2 - 3 - 4 -

4   4   5   5   4   4

Count:

Count:

Count: 1 - 2 - 3 - 4 -

Hot Cross Buns *

*See pages 104-107

Chapter II
Mary's Lamb

The tongue covers the 2nd, 3rd, 4th holes.

Draw

F

F is on the bottom space of the musical staff. It is the <u>DRAW</u> note in the fifth hole.

Written

F
5

Draw

⑰ Draw note F, hole 5

Count: 1 - 2 - 3 - 4   1 - 2 - 3 - 4 -   1 - 2 - 3 - 4 -   1 - 2 - 3 - 4
5   5   5   5   5   5   5   5

⑱

Count: 4   4   4   4   5   5   5   5

Count: 1 - 2 - 3 - 4 -

Count: 1 - 2 - 3 - 4 -

Dotted Half Note

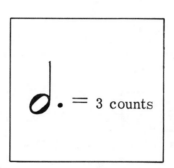

. = 3 counts

This is a dotted half note. In most music the dotted half note receives 3 counts.

One dotted half note has the value of 3 quarter notes.

Count: 1 - 2 - 3 - 4 -
Tap:

15

㉑

The tongue covers the 3rd, 4th and 5th holes.

Blow

G

G is on the second line of the musical staff. It is the **BLOW** note in the 6th hole.

Written

G

Blow

㉒ Blow in hole 6

Count: 1 - 2 - 3 - 4 - 1 - 2 - 3 - 4 - 1 - 2 - 3 - 4 - 1 - 2 - 3 - 4 - 1 - 2 - 3 - 4 -

㉓

Count: 1 - 2 - 3 - 4 -

Note Values

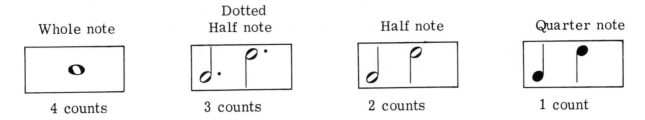

Whole note	Dotted Half note	Half note	Quarter note
4 counts	3 counts	2 counts	1 count

Fill in each box with the correct kind of note. Use ⬚Q for quarter note: ⬚H for the half note; ⬚DH for dotted half note; ⬚W for whole notes.

Fill in each box with the correct note value. (Number of counts)

Time Signature

Top number	**4**	= { Tells the number of Counts per measure }	=	**3** or **2**
Bottom number	**4**	= { Tells the kind of note that equals 1 count }	=	**4** or **4**

(24)

Count: 1 - 2 - 3 - 1 - 2 - 3 - 1 - 2 - 3 - 1 - 2 - 3 -
      4   4   5   5   6   5   4   4

(25)

Count: 1 - 2 - 1 - 2 - 1 - 2 - 1 - 2 - 1 - 2 -
      4   4   5   5   6   5   5   4   4

(26)

Count: 1 - 2 - 3 - 4 -
      4 4 5 5   6 5 6 5   6 5 5 4   5 5 4 4

IMPORTANT!
ALWAYS PLAY TO YOUR TAPPING.

Some Folks Do

Half Rest

Silence

2 counts

Written

Count: 1 - 2 -

In most music the
half rest recieves
$\frac{2}{=}$ counts of <u>Silence</u>.

Count: 1 - 2 -   3 - 4 -   1 - 2 - 3 - 4 -
⌐Silence⌐   6   5   4   4   ⌐Silence⌐   5

* Chords for Guitar accompaniment

First and second endings were created to shorten the printing of music.

I Know Where I'm Going

The Tie Note

The tie note is two or more notes of the same pitch that increase the length of sound.

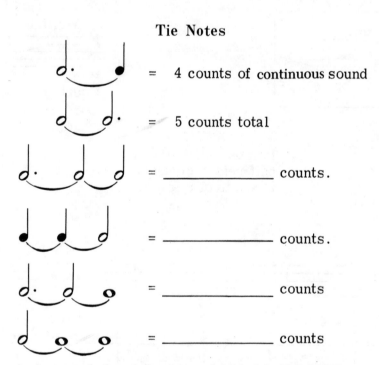

The first tie note is sounded and the second is held. <u>DO</u> <u>NOT</u> resound the second note, only hold it out for total value of both notes.

The first measure has only 3 counts. It begins with the second count. The first count may be found in the last measure.

When the Saints Go Marching In

Count: 2 - 3 - 4 -

Ode to Joy

Beethoven

Jingle Bells

Waltzing

Chapter III

The tongue covers the
3rd, 4th & 5th hole

Draw

A

A is on the second space of the musical staff. It is a __DRAW__ note on the 6th hole.

Written

A
6

Draw

Count: 1 - 2 - 3 - 4 - 1 - 2 - 3 - 4 -   1 - 2 - 3 - 4 -

Strawberry Roan

ALWAYS TAP YOUR FOOT!

Sanctus

F. Schubert

* Slurs: Two different notes to be played with one breath or played legato; not to be confused with tied notes of the same pitch.

Beautiful Brown Eyes

Look Down that Lonesome Road

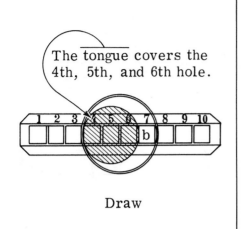

The tongue covers the 4th, 5th, and 6th hole.

Draw

B

B is on the 3rd line of the musical staff. It is a <u>DRAW</u> note in the 7th hole.

Written

B
7

Draw

Important:

Hole 4   Hole 5   Hole 6
Until now the pattern has been: Blow-Draw, Blow-Draw, Blow-Draw.
Hole 7
At the 7th hole this pattern is reversed; Draw-Blow.

(Reversed)

	Hole 4	Hole 5	Hole 6	Hole 7
Example:	Blow-Draw	Blow-Draw	Blow-Draw	Draw-Blow
	C d	E f	G a	b C

Draw in hole 7

Count: 1 - 2 - 3 - 4 -   1 - 2 - 3 - 4 -   1 - 2 - 3 - 4 -   1 - 2 - 3 - 4 -

Long, Long Ago

Chapter IV

The tongue covers the 4th, 5th, & 6th hole.

Blow

High **C**

C is on the 3rd space of the musical staff. It is a <u>BLOW</u> note on the 7th hole.

Written

High C
7

Blow

"C" Scale

Sweet Hour of Prayer

Little Annie Rooney

Billy Boy

The Marines' Hymn

How Can I Leave Thee

Drink to Me Only with Thine Eyes

Eighth Note

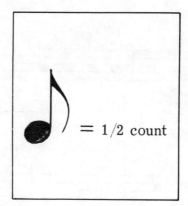

= 1/2 count

It takes
two eighth
notes=

to equal
one quarter
note=

The basic count or beat may be
sub-divided into TWO parts -
a down-beat and a up-beat

1 & 2 &   1 & 2 &   1 & 2 &   1 & 2 &

Count: 1 & 2 & 3 &4 &   1 & 2 & 3 &4 &   1 & 2 & 3 &4 &   1 & 2 & 3 & 4 &
6 6 6 6 6   6 6 6 6 6   6 6 6 6 6   6 6 6 6 6

Using the tapping foot you will recognize the <u>HALF</u> count when the
toe is up.

1   &   2   &   3   &

Minuet

J. S. Bach

Bach in Four

35

Alleluia

Blue Bells of Scotland

Sweet Betsy from Pike

Chapter V

Same value

Tied

Dotted Quarter Note

$1\frac{1}{2}$ counts

$\text{♩.} = 1\frac{1}{2}$ counts

Schubert's Waltz

She Wore a Yellow Ribbon

Whispering Hope

Alice Hawthorne

Joy to the World

G. F. Handel

French Folk Tune

Complete Silence

Count: 1 - 2 - 3 - 4 -   1 - 2 - 3 - 4 -   1 - 2 - 3 - 4 -   1 - 2 - 3 - 4 -

Resting in Three

A whole measure of rest

Count: 1 - 2 - 3 -   1 - 2 - 3 -

4 4 5   5 5 6   5   5 4 4 4   5 5 6

6 6 6   6 5 5   5 5 4   4 5 6   5 4

1 - 2 - 3 -

Strange Places

R. Schumann

5   7   7   7 6 6   5   7   7   7 6 6

5   7   6   6 5 5   4   6   5

43

Chapter VI

The tongue covers the 5th, 6th and 7th hole.

Draw

High

D

D is on the 4th line of the musical staff. It is on the 8th hole. It is a DRAW note.

Written

D
8
↓
Draw

⑲ Draw hole 8

Count: 1&2&3&4&
Tap: ↓↑↓↑↓↑↓↑

⑳

Count: 1-2-3-4- 1-2-3-4-

㉑

Count:

Country Gardens

English Folk Dance

Peer Gynt Suite

E. Grieg

Beethoven

Duet

Cowboy

Nobody Knows the Trouble I've Seen

Swanee River

The Drunken Sailor

Humoreske

Old Netherlands

50

While Shepherds Watched

G. F. Handel

I Gave My Love a Cherry

Count: 4   1 & 2 & 3 & 4 &

The Caisson Song

Eighth Rest

Chapter VII

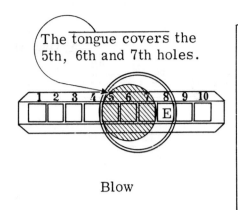

The tongue covers the 5th, 6th and 7th holes.

Blow

High

E

E is on the top space of the musical staff. It is on the 8th HOLE and is a __BLOW__ note.

Written

E
8
↑
Blow

⑨⑤ Blow note on hole 8

Count: 8   8 8   8 8 8 8   8 8 8 8 8 8 8 8   8

⑨⑥

Count: 7   8   8   8   7   8 8 8 8   7 7

⑨⑦

Count: 4 4 5 5   6 6 7 7   8 8 8 7   7 6 6 5   5 4 4 4

⑨⑧

Count: 4 4 5 5   4 5 5 6   5 5 6 6   5 6 6 7   6 6 7 7   6 7 7 8   7 7 8 8   7

Largo

A. Dvorak

Schumann Op. 68, No. 19

Old Time Religion

Worried Man Blues

Annie Laurie

Little Brown Jug

My Wild Irish Rose

America the Beautiful

Our Boys Will Shine Tonight

Wildwood Flower

Dixie

Chapter VIII

High

F

F is on the 5th line of the musical staff. It is a <u>DRAW</u> note on the 9th hole.

The tongue covers the 6th, 7th and 8th holes

Draw

Written

F
9
↓
Draw

⑩ Draw note on the 9th hole

Count: 1 – 2 – 3 – 4 –

⑪

Count: 1 – 2 – 3 – 4 –

⑫

Count: 1 & 2 &   1 & 2 &

Four by Four

⑬

Always tap your foot!

60

Alma Mater

Cielito Lindo

Johannes Brahms Op. 39, No. 2

Alleluia II

J. S. Bach

We Wish You a Merry Christmas

Swan Lake

Aura Lee

The Yellow Rose of Texas

Chapter IX

The tongue covers the 6th, 7th, and 8th hole

Blow

High

G

G is on the top of the musical staff. It is a **BLOW** note on the 9th hole.

Written

G
Blow
9

(122) Blow note in the 9th hole

Count: 1 & 2 & 3 & 4 &   1 & 2 &   3 & 4 &   1 & 2 & 3 & 4 &   1 & 2 & 3 & 4 &
Tap: ↓ ↑ ↓ ↑ ↓ ↑ ↓ ↑

9   9   9   9 9 9 9   9 9 9 9 9 9 9 9 9   9

(123)

Count: 4   5   6   7   8   9   9 8 8 7   7 6 6 5   5 4 4

(124)

4 5 4 5   5 6 5 6   6 7 6 7   7 8 7 8   8 9 8 9   9

Home on the Range

Sonata

W. A. Mozart

Birthday Party

Hail, Hail the Gang's All Here

Pathetique

P. I. Tchaikovsky

Red River Valley

The Triplet

La Boheme

Examination

1. A music staff is composed of _____ lines and _____ spaces.

2. Name the lines. _____

3. Name the spaces. _____

4. The top number in a time signature tells the _____ of counts

   in a _____ .

5. The lower number in a time signature tells the kind of a note

   that gets _____ count.

6. In $\frac{4}{4}$ time a whole note (𝐨) gets _____ counts.

7. In $\frac{3}{4}$ time a half note (𝅗𝅥) gets _____ counts.

8. The musical alphabet is composed of _____ letters. They

   are _____ .

9. When a piece begins with an incomplete measure, we find the

   remainder of the count in the _____ measure.

10. Rests are signs of _____ .

11. When two notes are tied (𝅗𝅥‿𝅗𝅥) should the second note be repeated?

    _____ .

12. Change the following notes to quarter notes.

13. When three note are placed together , they are

    called _____ .

71

Chapter X

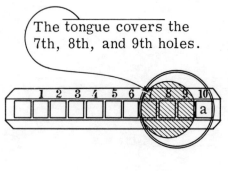

The tongue covers the 7th, 8th, and 9th holes.

Draw

High

A

A is on the first leger line above the musical staff.
It is a <u>DRAW</u> note in the 10th hole.

Written

A
10

Draw

(132)

Count: 1 & 2 & 3 & 4 & 1 & 2 & 3 & 4 &   1 & 2 & 3 & 4 &   1 & 2 & 3 & 4 &

10   10   10   10 10 10 10   10 10 10 10 10 10 10 10   10

(133)

4 4 5 5   6 6 7 7   8 8 9 9   10 9 9 8   8 7 7 6   6 5 5 4   4

(134)

4   5   6   7   8   9 10 9   8   7   6   5   4   5   6   7   6   5   4

72

God Rest Ye Merry, Gentleman

Nearer, My God, to Thee

Lowell Mason

Old Hundredth(1551)

Bourgeios

All Through the Night

Silent Night

America *

Looby Lou *

*Could be played one octave
lower, hole 4, 5 & 6.

Chapter XI

On the "C" harmonica there is no "B" note on the upper register.

The tongue covers the 7th, 8th, and 9th holes.

Blow

Double High

C

Double High C is on the second leger line above the musical staff. It is on the 10th hole and is a <u>BLOW</u> note.

Written

C
10

Blow

$\frac{4}{4}$ is the most "Common" time signature. Some times a "C" is used to express $\frac{4}{4}$ time.

(142)

Count: 1 - 2 - 3 - 4 -   1 - 2 - 3 - 4 -   1 - 2 - 3 - 4 -   1 - 2 - 3 - 4 -
   10   10   10   10 10 10 10   10

(143)

1-2- 3- 4-
4 4 5 5   6 6 7 7   8 8 9 9   10 10 10 9   9 8 8 7   7 6 6 5   5 4 4

(144) Cut-time / Alla-breve } means <u>TWICE</u> as fast (₵)

Written   Played   Written   Played   Written Played   Written Played
7 7 7 7   7 7 7 7   7   7   7   7   7 7   7 7   7   7

Battle Hymn of the Republic

"C" Harmonica

Large letters: Blow notes
Small letters: Draw notes

Turkey in the Straw

Chapter XII

The tongue covers the 1st and 2nd holes.

Draw

Low

B

Low B is below the first leger line below the musical staff. It is on the 3rd hole and is a <u>DRAW</u> note.

Written

B
3

Draw

(147) Draw note on hole 3

Count: 1 - 2 - 3 - 4 - 1 - 2 - 3 - 4 - 1 - 2 - 3 - 4 -
3   3   3   3   3   3   3   3

(148)

C   B   C   B
4   3   4   3

(149)

4   4   4   4   3   4   4   5   4   4   3   4

Mozart Sonata in C

Mendelssohn

La Spagnola

Mary Ann

Jesu, Joy of Man's Desiring

J. S. Bach

Chapter XIII

The tongue covers
hole one and two.

Blow

Low

G

G is below the musical staff, below 2 leger lines. It is a **BLOW** note in the 3rd hole of the harmonica.

Written

Second
G   leger
Blow line
3

(155) There is no "A" note in the lower register of the harmonica

Count: 1 &2&3&4&

Tap foot   1 & 2 & 3 & 4 &

Buffalo Gals

Oh, My Darling Clementine

William Tell

Rossini

Impromptu

F. Schubert
Op. 142, No. 2

Down in the Valley

Chapanecas

Alouette

Careless Love

O Christmas Tree

German

Bridal Chorus

R. Wagner

Boogie Woogie

Movin' on Boogie

Bounce Boogie

Stroll Boogie

Chapter XIV

When Johnny Comes Marching Home

House of the Rising Sun

Funny Times

Dance in Six – Eight

When the Dot is above or below the note it is a staccato. (A detached
or separated sound)

94

I Saw Three Ships

Traditional

Auprés de Ma Blonde

French Folk Tune

95

Jig

16th notes twice as fast as eigthth notes.

Moldau

B. Smetana

Harvest Song

Here We Come A – Wassailing

Chapter XV

The tongue covers the first hole only.

Draw

Low

G

Low G is below the second leger line below the staff. It is on the 2nd hole. It is a <u>DRAW</u> note.

Written

Second leger line

Draw

This note is usually used for <u>Blues</u>. Drawing the G note (in hole 2) as opposed the blowing the G note (in hole 3) allows blues players to use a"blues"technique called bending. However, it originally was used for the "G" chord (three notes played together). When drawing in holes 2, 3, and 4 you get the notes G-B-D. <u>That is the G chord</u>.

Example

Draw

G-Chord

There is <u>no "F" note</u> in the lower register of the harmonica.

Hole 1

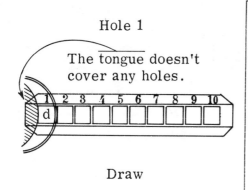

The tongue doesn't cover any holes.

Draw

Low

D

D is on the fourth leger line below the musical staff. It is in the first hole. It is a __DRAW__ note.

Written

Low D
4th leger line
1

(185) Draw in hole 1

Count: D
1   1   1   1 1 1 1   1

(186)

Draw	Draw	Draw	Blow
B	G	D	E
Hole	Hole	Hole	Hole
"3"	"2"	"1"	"2"

Count: 1 & 2 & 3 & 4 &
3   2   1   2

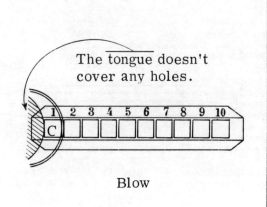

The tongue doesn't cover any holes.

Blow

Low

C

C is <u>below</u> the fourth leger line below the musical staff. It is in the first hole. It is a <u>BLOW</u> note.

Written

4th leger line

Low C

Low C

⑱⑦ Blow note in hole 1

⑱⑧ Blow

⑱⑨ Draw

102

Now <u>BLOW</u> into the bottom 4 holes without the tongue.

Example

Now <u>DRAW</u> into the bottom 4 holes without the tongue.

Example

Bottom Four Holes

Blow — Note & Chord

Use the tongue to cover holes 1, 2, & 3. Leave hole four open. Now release the tongue on holes 1, 2, & 3. Repeat.

Draw – Note & Chord

Use the tongue to cover holes 1, 2, & 3. Leave hole 4 open. Now release the tongue on hole 1, 2, & 3. Repeat.

Hot Cross Buns

Mary's Lamb

Quick release of the tongue, then back in position with the tongue.

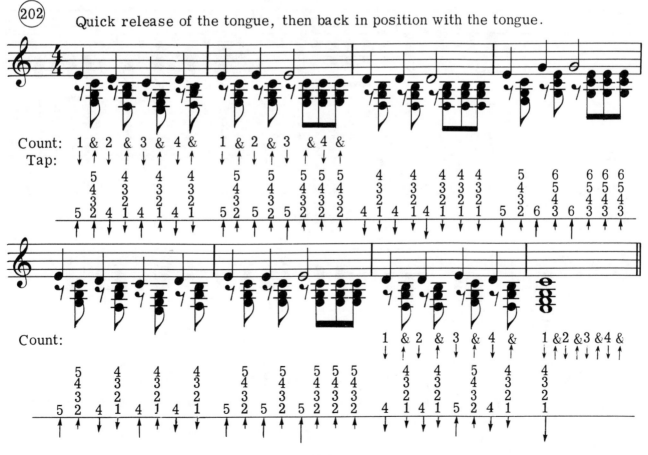

The following are excerpts from different songs. Four or more measures of examples of how to insert chords in different melodies. Examine the following then go back to your favorite tunes and interject these chords to suit your pleasure.

Way Down Upon the Swanee River

Exercise

Blue Bells of Scotland

Waltz

Great Music at Your Fingertips